Meow

A Day in the Life of Cats

JUDY REINEN

Megan Tingley Books

Little, Brown and Company
BOSTON NEW YORK LONDON

This book is dedicated to cats everywhere,

who show us the value of taking time out every day.

To my cats: Roady, Three Spot, Pancake, and Yabba Dabba Doo.

My inspirations!

Copyright © 2001 by Judy Reinen/Creative Shotz Photography Limited

First Edition

Library of Congress Cataloging-in-Publication Data

Reinen, Judy.
    Meow: a day in the life of cats / Judy Reinen.
        p. cm.
    Summary: Photographs depict cats in all sorts of human activities, from eating breakfast and taking a bath to going to school and reading a bedtime story.
    ISBN 0-316-83342-8
    [1. Cats — Fiction] I. Title.

PZ7.R27482 Cat 2001
[E]—dc21   00-062444

10 9 8 7 6 5 4 3 2 1

TWP

Printed in Singapore

This book features full-color photographs of live cats with sets designed and photographed by Judy Reinen. The breeds featured on each page are as follows: Title page, domestic; page 3, British shorthair; page 4, black (moggy) domestic; page 5, domestic; page 6, domestic; pages 7 and 8, Birman; page 9, Burmese; pages 10 and 11, (l. to r.) two Persians and one British; page 12, British shorthair; page 13, Persian; page 14, black-and-white domestic; page 15, two ginger and one tabby domestic; page 16, Persian; page 17, Birman; page 18, multicolored domestic; page 19, Persian; page 20, black-and-white domestic; page 21, British; page 22, domestic; page 23, (l. to r.) black, tortoiseshell, multicolored domestic; page 24, tabby domestic; page 25, Rex; page 26, Persian; page 27, domestic; page 28, ginger domestic; page 29, color point Persian; page 31, Birman; page 32, British shorthair.

A big thank-you to the owners of all the cats I have had the privilege of capturing on film.
Your enthusiasm and support are greatly appreciated.
—J. R.

Have you ever wondered what cats do all day?
You probably think we just eat and sleep.
Actually, a cat's day is just like yours!
We took these pictures to show you....

We like to sleep late...

but you are always waking us up.

We start the day with a big stretch.

And a good
scratch.

Then we have a healthy breakfast.

And check
the mail.

Cats like to be
very clean...

so we take
a very long
bath.

Then we go off to school.

We like to find lots of new places to hang out.

We always like a nice glass of milk.
We try to keep it all to ourselves...

but sometimes
we have to
share.

We fix a lot of important things around the house.

And make it look pretty.

we keep an eye on the pets...

and make sure they get fresh air.

We love to knit...

but it's so tiring!

We're a big help in the garden.

Sometimes we go fishing...

and then make a tasty fishy snack.

When it's time to go out, we do our hair...

and get dressed up.

We
love to
eat...

(Can you
guess
what our
favorite
food is?)

but don't like to cook.

A FELINE GUIDE TO
HOLIDAY HOT SPOTS

CAT PSYCHOLOGY

FASHION CATTERLEY   *Tribute to Spring*

GROOM!   JR

HOW TO CLAW YOUR WAY TO THE TOP

FLEAS AND FURBALLS   Dr. Freddy F. Fish

YARN & ITS MEANING TO YOU

HOW TO TRAIN YOUR DOG.   Kit E. Kat

Canaries and You. A family guide.   by Bud & Jerry Garr

THE LOST ART OF WHISKER GROOMING   FLYING FUR PRESS

WORLD CATLAS

Why cats are smarter than dogs

LOOKING OUT THE CAT DOOR: A RETROSPECTIVE   F.E. LINE

LEARNING TO MEOW IN PORTUGUESE

After dinner, we read a bedtime story.

You & the Modern Cat

Judy Reinen

You and the
Modern Cat

And go to sleep...
just like you.